NEW KIDS ON THE BLOCK SCRAPBOOK

BY **ANNE M. RASO**,
EDITOR, *Teen Dream* MAGAZINE

Donnie Wahlberg, Jonathan Knight, Joe McIntyre, Jordan Knight and Danny Wood (left to right) in New York's Central Park. *Robin Platzer*

Modern Publishing
A Division of Unisystems, Inc.
New York, New York 10022

Front Cover Photo by Chris Mackie
Book Design by Bob Feldgus

CONTENTS

NKOTB at the Palladium in New York for radio station Z-100's Sixth Annual Anniversary Party.
Robin Platzer

Jon Knight arriving at the 32nd Annual Grammy Awards in Los Angeles.
Scott Downie, Celebrity Photo

Joe, Donnie and Jordan arriving at Los Angeles Airport for the Grammy Awards.
Janet Gough, Celebrity Photo

The New Kids On The Block presenting an award at the 32nd Annual Grammy Awards in Los Angeles.
Ken Sax Photography

BEANTOWN BOYS MAKE GOOD!

It's been almost two years since those darlin' dudes from Beantown—Donnie Wahlberg, Danny Wood, Jon Knight, Jordan Knight and Joe McIntyre hit the "big time." The turning point for them was their tour with Tiffany in Summer '88, giving them just the exposure they needed. In just a few short months after that tour, Tiffany and the New Kids reversed roles—suddenly she was their warm-up act, and Tiffany soon found herself under the wing of the New Kids' legendary manager, Dick Scott, and producer Maurice Starr (who also put together those other boys from Beantown, New Edition).

Have the boys changed since they hit the top with the multiple-hit LP, *Hangin' Tough* (a *Billboard* Top 10 for over a year)? NO! Judy McIntyre,

Joe's oldest sister, reports, "Joe is still the nice, sweet, generous, funny, cuddly kid he's always been. He still laughs and jokes and kids around the way he did when he was twelve years old—which wasn't so long ago. The only changes in Joe are the changes that come with getting older."

At any show in Boston or New York, you can find members from almost every New Kid clan—sometimes even including aunts, uncles and cousins.

Danny's mom, Betty Wood, probably was the most leery of her son joining a pop group. After all, Danny was academically inclined and already attending his first semester at Boston University (on full scholarship!) when *Hangin' Tough*

The guys say they "...plan to stay together for as long as possible..."
Vinnie Zuffante, Star File Photo

Jon, Joe, Donnie and Danny (left to right) in action on stage during a performance.
David Seelig, Star File Photo

was being recorded. She even asked the dean to encourage Danny to stay in school and forget pop stardom (she was hoping he'd become an architect or engineer). But the dean told her, "If you don't let your son stay with the group, he'll always wonder 'What if…?' and that would affect his achievement in the future." Mrs. Wood heeded the dean's advice, and Danny even credited the dean on the

Hangin' Tough album. (Yes, Danny still keeps in touch!)

This book is not just another New Kids bio—it's a handbook filled with fun photos and info about the goings-on in the New Kids camp. Whether the book surprises you, inspires you, or makes you laugh, one thing is certain—you won't be bored for a single minute! Wherever the New Kids are, fun is bound to follow!

THE HARDEST WORKING KIDS IN SHOW BUSINESS

The New Kids On The Block often are referred to as "The Hardest Working Kids In Show Business." Ben Vereen even introduced them that way on the recent United Cerebral Palsy Telethon. Unlike some of the other megastar rockers, the New Kids will play a major venue (which seats 15,000 or more) at least four times a year. Even the Rolling Stones only play the same market twice in a year—so that tells you something about the New Kids' popularity!

What drives the boys to work so hard when they easily could sit back on their duffs three or four months out of the year, and rely on their album and singles success to "snowball" as they have for the past eighteen or so months? Because they love what they do, pure and simple.

"Well, the best part of all this is just being able to go onstage in front of 20,000 people every night and perform and hear all the girls screaming and every-thing," Donnie remarked during a press conference in Atlanta last year. "I also love going into the studio and recording and just hangin' out—the five of us—and being together."

However, Donnie also points out the downside to fame: "We don't have too much of a private life anymore. The most time we have alone is at night in a hotel room."

Joe's sister says, "Joe is still the nice, sweet, generous, funny, cuddly kid he's always been." *Chris Mackie*

"Even then," Jon adds, "kids still find out our hotel numbers, and they still call us on the phone all night."

But the guys are more than willing to deal with these invasions of privacy because the positives far outweigh the negatives when it comes to being famous. Jon talks about how nice it feels to be so well-traveled at a young age: "Most kids our age don't even get out of their own neighborhoods, and we've been to London twice, Japan three times, Amsterdam once. We have plans to tour Europe again, and we've been in 49 out of 50 states!"

Even Joe, the least adventurous member of the group, now admits that he also loves the traveling. He reveals, while tugging on his newly-permed golden locks, "At first I didn't like going to different countries. I mean, I couldn't wait to get back to the States, but traveling is getting better and better."

Jon chimes in, "And it's cool being in England 'cause at least everybody speaks English. When you go to Japan, you can't walk into McDonald's and order a Big Mac unless somebody's with you, so you feel really far away then."

Besides traveling, the guys also have been branching off into cartoonland. Yep, the New Kids On The Block cartoon (at press time simply called *New Kids On The Block*), is due to

Danny's got a "live and let live" philosophy toward life. *Ernie Paniccioli*

Place your favorite photo here

premiere on ABC Saturday mornings in September. Comments Joe, "We're really looking forward to doing the cartoon—and we hope to be using our own voices. We feel that it would kind of be a gyp otherwise."

And what kind of adventures will the New Kids go on in their new cartoon series? "Sort of the same adventures we go on in real life—only exaggerated," says Joe. "A lot of the stories will be based on what really goes on—the screaming girls, the concerts, recording—but we'll be getting into mischievous situations. Stuff will happen like in The Beatles and Jackson Five cartoons, only it will be the '90s. This should be a real high-tech cartoon."

The battle over who would produce the New Kids' cartoon was all over the *Hollywood Reporter* last fall before DIC, the major animation company, won out. How much the New Kids got for the deal was kept hush-hush by manager Dick Scott, but it was over a cool million.

Almost constant TV appearances also have been keeping the New Kids busy. They have been guests on *The Arsenio Hall Show* (during the second taping, the only other guest was Robert DeNiro, which thrilled Donnie), *The United Cerebral Palsy Telethon* (which they've participated in for four years now), *The Joe Franklin Show* (a popular talk show in the New York City area), *The*

Jon, the oldest New Kid, is like a big brother to the group. *Vinnie Zuffante, Star File Photo*

New Mickey Mouse Club, and their own self-titled Disney Channel special which was a live concert with many special guests (including Milli Vanilli and Tiffany).

Due to the success of the New Kids' Christmas album, *Merry, Merry Christmas*, ABC-TV has offered them a Christmas special to be aired during the 1990 Christmas season and manager Dick Scott has already been consulting with producer Maurice Starr about the material the guys will be performing. Expect a lot of the glitz displayed during the special Christmas portion of their most recent concerts where Jordan dressed up as a guitar-playing Santa Claus and the guys donned Liberace-like sequined suits for a beautiful, traditional Christmas song medley.

"We had a lot of fun doing the Christmas album," says Jordan. "We got to sing a lot of our old favorites—like "The Christmas Song (Chestnuts Roasting On an Open Fire)"—and new songs that were written just for us, like "This One's For The Children." That song could have been recorded any time of year.

"The Christmas songs have always been special to us," Jordan continues, "and to be able to take it one step further by doing a whole Christmas thing onstage was really special."

Jon talks about the very first time they did the Christmas

Appreciative fans throw flowers and teddy bears onstage after every show. *Chris Mackie*

segment live in concert. "It's funny—the first night we did the show like that, me and Joe were sitting back there onstage laughing so hard 'cause Danny came out with this wig on. We couldn't even sing, we were laughing so hard!"

In addition to the Christmas special and other TV appearances, Disney has a feature film in the works for them. Though the guys can't start on it until they get back from their European tour this summer, they've already started making suggestions to the screenplay writers. All that is known at press time is that the guys hope to have the film out in early '91 and that they do not play themselves.

"I'm not supposed to talk about it yet," says Joe. "It's still in negotiations, but I think it will have a little of everything— action, adventure and comedy."

It's obvious that the New Kids' fans have an eyeful and an earful comin' at them in the next year—not to mention the New Kids dolls and other paraphernalia that will be hitting the toy market in August and their next LP! It seems it's the New Kids' world…and we all just live in it.

Donnie's fascination with Michael Jackson sparked his interest in music.
Ernie Paniccioli

SIZZLING IN THE STUDIO

The New Kids' latest album, *Step By Step*, scheduled for a May 8 release, will also be produced by Maurice Starr.

Joe McIntyre talked about the new album during a record company bash held in Rockefeller Center right around Christmastime. "We're going for that classic sound," he remarked. "Our songs are songs that are ageless and timeless. Did you know that "Please Don't Go Girl" was written twenty years ago—back when Maurice was only fifteen?

He's got a huge catalog of songs that we pull from. And every last song is a classic. All I can say about the new album is that it's got a classic sound—and that Donnie, Jordan, and Danny did their Crickets thing again." (In case you don't know, The Crickets are a spin-off of the New Kids—it's the team that Donnie, Jordan, and Danny formed so they could produce, write songs, and engineer, respectively).

The guys, known as the hardest working kids in show business, absolutely love to perform.
Ebet Roberts

The amazing thing about the forthcoming album is that most of the vocals were recorded in hotel rooms. Dick Scott had microphones, consoles, and other recording equipment set up in the guys' rooms so that they could record vocal tracks during their free time. And when the guys got more than a few hours free, they went to an actual recording studio (for instance, Jordan and Donnie did some work in an Atlanta studio last November). But when the album actually hits your turntable this spring, you can bet that it'll sound just like one that's been recorded in a studio over a two or three month period.

Do the guys feel pressure to top the 10 million-plus sales of *Hangin' Tough* or the quadru-ple-platinum sales of their Christmas album? Jon replies, "We can't make anything hap-pen, but judging from the buzz on the Christmas album and from the things I hear from talk-ing to the fans, I get good vibes that the next record will be a success. Will it top *Hangin' Tough*? It's hard to top album sales of 10 million—but we'll settle for *half* that this time around!"

Donnie says, "We do what we want to do for ourselves—and we figure that if we like it, the fans will like it. We've done our best and I hope the fans will see that."

Jordan's mom calls him her "enchanted one."
Mike Quastella, Star File Photo

Place your favorite photo here

Place your favorite photo here

The Kids hope that their newest album, *Step By Step,* will be as popular as *Hangin' Tough.* Bob Gruen, *Star File Photo*

Jordan and Jon with their close friend, Debbie Gibson.
Vinnie Zuffante, Star File Photo

Jordan with Robo, one of the New Kids' bodyguards.
Ernie Paniccioli

LIVING DOLLS

Can you imagine what it would be like to have a doll made in your likeness? Well, a marketing genius at Hasbro Toys realized that New Kids dolls would be one hot item. The dolls and other NKOTB products were previewed for the first time at a special press conference before the annual New York Toy Fair in February.

When word leaked out through a radio station that the New Kids would be appearing at this press conference held at New York's Hard Rock Cafe, over one thousand fans gathered in less than two hours! Waving at TV cameras, sporting New Kids tour jackets, and waving banners, the fans professed their love for certain members of the group, and asked reporters and photogra-

Cheering fans show off their New Kids paraphernalia.
Robin Platzer

phers on their way inside to give flowers or gifts to the boys. A few particularly bold gals simply jotted their phone numbers on a piece of paper and passed them to members of the press.

NKOTB dolls, stage set and accessories due on the market in August, 1990. *Courtesy of Hasbro Toys, Inc.*

Somehow, the guys got through this tremendous crowd—held in check by approximately twenty NYC cops—without a hair out of place, although Joe did admit that the scene made him a little nervous.

Once inside, the Kids hung out on the mezzanine while reporters and photographers took the seats set up for them downstairs. The dolls were arranged on a table along with the rest of the Hasbro NKOTB

The "living dolls" presenting their dolls at New York's Hard Rock Cafe. *Robin Platzer*

Place your favorite photo here

line, which includes a 2′ high mini-stage with accessories, poster puzzles, and a line of electronics.

When the guys made their way down the famous red staircase holding their respective dolls, the president of Hasbro beamed while the crowd stood and cheered. When asked what it was like to see little life-like replicas of themselves, Danny responded: "It's pretty cool. They really did a great job, though I never thought of myself as being this short." (The dolls are only 12¼″ high).

However, some of the questions were tougher. For example, one reporter asked if the dolls would hurt their careers— implying that audiences would take the NKOTB music less seriously with dolls on the market.

"Well," Donnie replied, "Michael Jackson was twenty-nine when his doll came out and it certainly didn't make anyone take his music less seriously."

The Kids couldn't be more handsome than they were at the television taping for the Grammy Living Legend Award. *Vinnie Zuffante, Star File Photo*

Will the New Kids dolls and other merchandise sell? Without a doubt! Toy stores around the country already have their orders in, and as one buyer whispered to a member of the press: "This line is going to blow the toy market wide open this year."

Announcing the doll line was one of the Kids' proudest moments. And who got to keep the dolls they were gifted with that day? Each guy carefully tucked his doll in his suitcase to give to his mom.

"I'm giving my doll to my mother because she's a living doll," said Danny. "Without her, I wouldn't be here today. Here's a message to all New Kids fans: Be good to your mom!"

Joe, the youngest Kid, turns up at the top of popularity polls conducted by dozens of teen magazines.
Ernie Paniccioli

Place your favorite photo here

JORDAN KNIGHT DOES IT RIGHT

Marlene Knight has always referred to son Jordan as her "enchanted one," and fans around the world certainly will agree with that description.

wavy brown hair —

dreamy brown eyes —

enchanting smile —

But Jonathan's view of Jordan is a little less idyllic than their mother's. "Jordan's not only my brother—he's my best friend, but we do have our disagreements," says Jonathan. "When you're around anyone for 24 hours a day that's just what it's like. Jordan can be very blunt, too—if you look ugly one day, he'll tell you that to your face. It's not that he's mean. He's just very honest. But you can trust him with anything. He always comes through for you. I wish I could pick up some of his better qualities."

Jordan is basically just a good old Boston boy (well, actually he's from the lovely suburb of Dorchester). He started singing when he was in sixth grade when Jon recruited him into the local church choir and he's been singing ever since.

When the brothers were recruited into the group back in 1984 by producer Maurice Starr and his assistant Mary Alford, Mrs. Knight panicked. While she wanted her sons to follow their dreams, she also knew that they were quite young and easily could be sucked into the pitfalls of showbiz. Still, she knew they were good kids and that coming from a big family had taught them to be considerate of others and to feel strength in their individuality.

Mrs. Knight says, "I felt sorry for them when their friends would be out working part-time jobs and making money to go out on dates and have fun, and they would be down in the basement rehearsing. I felt like they were giving up the best years of their lives."

Obviously, all that hard work paid off. "There were times I felt discouraged," explains Jordan, "but I knew that someday it would all come together. We had a lot of faith in Maurice. He already had an impressive track record with New Edition and worked hard on getting us a record deal. Within a year or two, we were signed with Columbia Records—the biggest record company in the world. We knew you needed more than a major recording contract to make it, but the faith was there. It was almost like a club between the five of us and Maurice, and he always gave

Place your favorite photo here

us words of encouragement when we had to skip a party and stay in and learn a new dance step or song.

"My mother was a little upset that we weren't doing the normal things that kids our age do, but we assured her that we were having fun, and that someday we'd make it. Unfortunately, she had heard stories about kids who went into show business and turned all bratty and got into trouble. She finally laid back and let things be... and it all worked out. She's our biggest fan."

Jordan is the hearthrob of the New Kids and his handsome, young Elvis Presley-type looks are the most popular with concert audiences.

Jordan describes himself this way: "I have typical tastes for a guy my age and I like doing all the typical stuff like playing basketball and meeting girls."

Did you say "girls"? Now that's an interesting subject. We asked him if he would ever date a fan. After a bit of thought, he responded, "Yes, I would. They couldn't be that type of fan who screams and goes crazy. I want someone who can appreciate what we do and enjoy it, but have a mature attitude about it. She would have to like me for *me*—not for the star she thinks I am. That is only an illusion."

Jordan's hopes for the future include seeing the New Kids stay on top. He's eagerly awaiting the New Kids movie and

Christmas special and hopes that they will help the group venture out into acting roles. "My secret dream is to be in a movie with Eddie Murphy—but please don't repeat that in front of the other guys, they might laugh at me! I guess that's aiming a little too high for a guy that's never acted before. I think all of us are really funny though—all natural comedians. But singing will always come first."

Jordan's idea of a good night is just being at home and being able to get away from all the chaos on the road—not that he doesn't love the road. His mom reveals, "When the boys come home, they just want to be treated like they've always

Jordan, often compared to Elvis Presley, is the heartthrob of the New Kids. *Vinnie Zuffante, Star File Photo*

been. They don't even want the name 'New Kids' uttered at all. It disturbs them when they see fans looking in their bedroom windows or when a few particularly aggressive fans ring the doorbell. They want to be left alone entirely."

On a national morning talk show a year ago Jordan mentioned that fans were coming up to his family's house and stealing twigs. He said he couldn't believe anyone would do such a thing.

Jordan says he's just a "typical" guy who likes doing typical things like playing basketball and meeting girls.
Vinnie Zuffante, Star File Photo

Jordan and Jon worry about their mom when they're away. *Robin Platzer*

"Well, that made the situation even worse," says Jon. "People were taking whole branches and bags of leaves. Fortunately, my mother's attitude is, 'Well, I have three-quarters of an acre, so missing a little bit of grass won't be too bad.' If any of you are listening out there, I would appreciate it if you stayed off our lawn. I want my mother to feel safe. I admit, I worry about her when we're away."

Mrs. Knight is in the front row of every Boston and New York–area show cheering her boys on. "When I see them onstage, I feel so proud. In a way, it's funny because they just seem like regular guys. But I can put myself into those screaming girls' shoes and see what they see in my sons."

And what does Jordan have to say about his crazy life? "It's not totally crazy—we're five kids who are totally *normal* made to live a crazy existence. But we handle the fame thing. We know it could all be gone tomorrow, but with the love and blessings of our fans, we'll be around for awhile. And we'll be doing everything to keep it going."

Jordan's secret dream is to be in a movie with Eddie Murphy.
Vinnie Zuffante, Star File Photo

JONATHAN KNIGHT: LIKE NIGHT AND DAY!

Jonathan Knight is known not only for being the oldest member of the New Kids (he turns twenty-two on November 29), but as the quietest member of the group. But describe Jonathan as the "quiet one," and brother Jordan is bound to dispute it.

wonderful brown hair

thoughtful hazel eyes

look at those lashes!

mysterious smile

"Jonathan can get as crazy as the rest of us, especially after a long night on the tour bus. Other people just don't get to know what he's really like—you really have to be an old friend or be around him all the time," says Jordan. "Jonathan's a good guy—he's like the big brother of the group. He tells us to mind our manners and keep our elbows off the table. He's the real gentleman of the group, but there's a time when—pardon the pun—he's like night and day."

Marlene Knight simply describes Jonathan as "her loving son." Mrs. Knight always gets a hug or kiss before show-time, and that makes her happy. "If I didn't think Jonathan was emotionally mature, I wouldn't have let him join the group. Sure, I worried at first, but he's a good kid and he knows I trust him. I only get upset when he's lost ten or fifteen pounds when he comes off the road after three or so months. I never treat my sons like babies, but when I see Jonathan looking like that, I want to ply him with dozens of cookies and milk as if he was six years old!"

Jonathan is a little less likely to go up to strangers than the rest of the boys, and tends to kind of stand back and size up the person silently. Jon discusses his attitude towards strangers—and he has to deal with *a lot* of strangers who approach him for autographs or photo opportunities. "I really

Place your favorite photo here

like people, it's just that sometimes you're a little scared. I've read about the trouble crazy fans have caused for some celebrities and I'm a little concerned. Now, our fans are 99½ percent terrific, but you never know. I want to kind of size someone up before I talk to them."

How does a shy guy like Jon handle dozens of girls walking up to his house—and standing in his driveway or even peering in his bedroom window? Well, at first he was shocked. He had no idea that he would ever be this famous or that anyone would ever be so interested in him.

Jon's "soft" good looks—as contrasted to his brother Jordan's dramatic good looks—have captured many a heart, but he never realized he was cute until female fans started going crazy over him. It's really nice that neither of the Knight brothers have become vain despite girls going to crazy lengths to meet them. And even nicer is the fact that the brothers' relationship has grown closer with time and touring. The closeness in their ages might've caused a conflict when they were much younger, but today they are the best of friends.

Coming from a big family has also helped Jonathan to get along with people and he trusts people more as he gets to know them better. Jon remembers first enjoying being with large groups of people when he was a member of the local church choir with Jordan. To this day, Jon remembers many of the hymns, and a little bit of the gospel singing style is evident in the way he performs today.

Jonathan is rather sentimental. One of his fondest memories is going to his grandma's summer home in Ontario and wearing the little Toronto Maple Leafs uniform she bought him when he was a preschooler. "We were always close to our grandparents," says Jonathan. "They pretty much let us do what we wanted at their summer home. And we got to eat lots of popsicles and chase after frogs."

What is Jonathan's philosophy toward life now that he's a full-fledged adult? "I just take things one day at a time, and I believe that if you treat people the way *you* want to be treated, they'll treat you the right way. All of us are concerned about today's racial problems though we were all raised in mixed neighborhoods and never really saw any racial problems up-close and firsthand. Every-

Jon and his Shar-Pei puppy, Houston— Jon's most constant escort.
Chris Mackie

one got along great, at least in my neighborhood. People are all the same, no matter what color their skin is. They all want to be happy and they want to be loved and respected."

Jonathan spreads his message of peace everytime he gets onstage. Although it may sound corny, Jon often tells the audience to "love one another." And though he enjoys the teddy bears, signs, and banners the fans throw onstage at the end of the show, he likes the flowers the best. He'll often grab a bunch at the end of the show and take them back to the dressing room. But if he can't find a vase or glass to put the flowers in, he gives them to fans who were lucky enough to get backstage.

Jon's favorite thing about fame is getting to travel and live an interesting life. He loves not having to worry about what town he's in. "Life on the road is like one big traveling circus. We're not spoiled or pampered, but we enjoy staying in nice hotels and getting to live kind of 'off' hours. We're always so busy and could easily spend 24 hours a day doing stuff—like signing autographs or going on talk shows or the news—but we try to be selective. We need a few hours a day to collect our thoughts and mentally prepare for the show.

"Getting ready for a show really is an entire process. It's like you have to clear your head of any negative thoughts and focus them all on doing our best out there. We think: 'The crowd is really going to be blown away. They're really going to be happy.' You have this self-fulfilling prophecy that you're going to do your best.

"I admit I get a little nervous right before we go on. I try to smile and tell myself that everything is going to be fine, though. And Robo and Biscuit —our bodyguards—give us the 'high five' and push us to do our best. They're almost like managers sometimes. They're definitely there to support us more than just protect us. They're even there for the little things. Like if I'm walking my Shar-Pei puppy Houston—which Biscuit always calls Kiko for some reason—and it's time to go on, one of them will take Houston on the rest of his walk. They're there to do things big and small and provide emotional support. You couldn't ask for better guys. They look scary, but they're just like these big human teddy bears."

Speaking of Houston, he's Jonathan's most constant escort. Unfortunately, the New Kids' busy touring and recording schedule doesn't allow time for girlfriends—or even dating for that matter. Jon says his favorite qualities in a girl are "independence and understanding," and he points out that being a NKOTB fan doesn't hurt, either.

How would you sum up Jon Knight? How about 'a loving, warm, older brother type who takes care of those around him.' Yep, he's special...a real "Knight in shining armor"!

Jon at Tiffany's 18th birthday party in Los Angeles.
Vinnie Zuffante, Star File Photo

HANGIN' TOUGH WITH DONNIE WAHLBERG

Donnie Wahlberg is the kind of guy you wished you had as a big brother. He's got something clever to say for every situation, and he loves slapstick humor.

sun-streaked blond hair

sensitive hazel eyes

tender mouth

Ernie Paniccioli

Though he's the most quick-witted of the New Kids, he can be a bit of a smart aleck. But Donnie's sensitive and intense under that playful exterior.

"People don't always understand me, but they want to be my friend. I like to think that I can put a smile on anyone's face. I sincerely want all people to be happy. Life is too short to be unhappy," he philosophizes.

Donnie's mom, Alma, says that she always knew that her son would become somebody. She reveals, "I always knew he was different from the other kids. Always. He demanded attention. When he spoke, everyone had to listen. He loved music, he loved the drums—he was always banging around on things. He was very creative. He loved to draw and write stories. He had a great imagination."

Donnie's fascination with Michael Jackson sparked his interest in music. His mom says he would always moonwalk through the house, and when it came time to audition for New Kids On The Block in 1984, he did a lengthy impersonation of "The Gloved One" for Maurice Starr and Mary Alford. (Prior to auditioning for NKOTB, he entered a couple of talent shows impersonating Michael Jackson.)

Despite Donnie's obvious talent, Alma Wahlberg Conroy did not want her son going into show business. "I was scared," she explains. "I really wanted Donnie to finish school. I was

Place your favorite photo here

also nervous about him being away from home; being with people that I didn't know. I wanted to be very involved, so I went to every rehearsal, every neighborhood show. I was there every time they performed until I started to feel secure about the people they were dealing with. They really cared about him, and Donnie proved to me that he could do his schooling, sing with the group, and have a part-time job. He did well at all three!"

During the early New Kids days, Donnie worked in a bank and at a shoe store, proud to be juggling his part-time jobs along with all his other goings-on. He eventually did give up his jobs when the New Kids got their recording contract and recorded their first album (which was self-titled). From that point, the guys got fairly regular concert work even if

they weren't being paid much. Early on, they did a lot of gigs simply to be seen and gather publicity—performing at Boston's Kite Festival and at the Liberty Island Fourth of July festivities in 1986.

Donnie's mom loved watching the group's popularity grow in the period between the release of their first album in March '87, and when *Hangin Tough* came out the next year. And when the guys opened for Tiffany during Summer '88, making the NKOTB the most-talked-about group in teendom, Alma Wahlberg Conroy was bursting with pride.

Donnie's success has brightened her life and she's proud to say that he hasn't changed. "The part I enjoy the most is the fans. I love going to the shows and watching the audience. I always go over and talk to the girls—to me, that's the most exciting part. When I get fan mail, I can relate to a lot of these kids. I'm kind of uncomfortable meeting the higher-up people, like from CBS, but I'm very comfortable on the fans' level. I really love it."

And Donnie loves it, too. "I wouldn't change places with anyone else in the world," says Donnie (who was oddly nicknamed "Cheese" by the other boys). "It's such an intense vibe to hear all the girls screaming and seeing all these flashbulbs go off in your face."

But success goes a lot deeper than just crazed fans for Donnie. "You know, it feels good to have accomplished what we have. We've been doing this almost six years and it's helped us acquire self-discipline and self-respect. You know, this wasn't handed to us on a silver platter. I can't totally explain this but I really feel like somebody and that makes me feel good."

Donnie and the guys have grown closer and that makes him happy, too. "When you've got the same guys in your face all the time, it's not easy—unless they're the four guys I work with. The chemistry is there and we feel really comfortable with each other. I don't think I could feel as comfortable with anyone else in the whole world. I'm not just saying that 'cause it looks good to the press that we get along. I sincerely love these guys like brothers, and I believe in their talents as well. I think they've only begun to shine."

Not surprisingly, the theme of a painting Donnie did when he was sixteen (yes, he is also an amateur but very talented artist) was entitled "Changes Don't Affect True Friends," for which he won a prize from his high school art department.

Donnie also liked writing in high school and won a prize for an essay about friendship. "I've always loved to be creative. It's the way I let out the energy pent up inside me. Believe it or not, being onstage is not enough for me—I've got to work overtime in the recording studio producing, and now I even have a group of friends I work with, The Northside Boys. More than anything in the world, I want them to make it big."

Donnie says the downside to fame is the lack of privacy, but he wouldn't change places with anyone else in the world.
Ernie Paniccioli

Donnie has modeled himself after Maurice Starr, whom he always admired for his songwriting track record, and for so artfully masterminding New Edition and the New Kids On The Block. "Maurice is our main man. If you ever hear rumors that we don't get along or any of that silly stuff—forget it. Maurice is like one of us. We're lucky that he has always worked with us so closely. I mean, we were nobodies when he discovered us. He molded us into what we are today, and he's still there guiding us 100 percent of the way.

"I watched this wizard at work and have tried to absorb as much of his talents as possible—but if I'm ever *half* as talented as him, I'll be happy."

According to Donnie's mom, his unpredictability is one of his strongest characteristics, just one of the things that makes him lovable. His mom likes to tell the story about how he snuck back into B-Town at 3:00 a.m. one morning when he was recording their latest album. Alma Wahlberg Conroy was shocked when she found her son in the kitchen drinking orange juice and eating Minute rice (it was the clinks and clanks of the pan being put onto the stove that woke her up). The key word to knowing Donnie Wahlberg is "surprise"—you just never know what this lovable kid is going to pull next. And now that he's talking about going into acting as a sideline to singing—well, this living legend will be larger than life!

Place your favorite photo here

DANNY WOOD, THE LITTLE BOY WHO COULD!

Danny Wood is half-Portuguese and his thick black locks and dark brown eyes are enough to send any girl out of her mind. But probably the

lustrous black hair ————

mischievous brown eyes ————

warm, inviting smile ————

most fetching thing about "Puff McCloud" (as he is affectionately called by the other Kids) is that he is an exceptional dancer. Danny, along with NKOTB choreographer Tyrone Procter, thinks up all those original dance moves.

As a matter of fact, Danny's favorite part of the New Kids show is when he gets to breakdance. If you ever wonder why Danny always wears such baggy pants—well, he *needs* to wear them to perform those incredible moves. When he tried doing them in tight pants, they ripped and he had a rather embarrassing moment!

Danny confesses that as a child, he was rather mischievous. But his mom, Betty, disagrees. "He did everything he put his mind to, and he was bright beyond his years. Even as a child, he was that strong silent type. He could be quiet and listen to what everyone had to say about a certain situation—then assess it and summarize it for everyone. He was kind of like the peacemaker between the kids in the neighborhood. He was quiet, but he was also assertive. He wasn't afraid to take risks.

"When I think about Danny as a child, I think mainly about how he was very academically gifted. All the teachers loved him and one always talked about how she loved his big brown eyes. She said he was going to be a real heartbreaker someday. And she was right!"

Even today, Donnie says,

"Danny is the kind of guy who'll see a job through from start to finish. He never lets anything go. Once he starts it, you can count on him to finish it. He's a great organizer, and he's very enthusiastic. The rest of us always put our heads up to Danny's before a show hoping that his energy level will transfer to us via osmosis."

Mrs. Wood *does* worry about Danny when he's on tour…is he eating O.K., is he overworking himself? "But I do see that

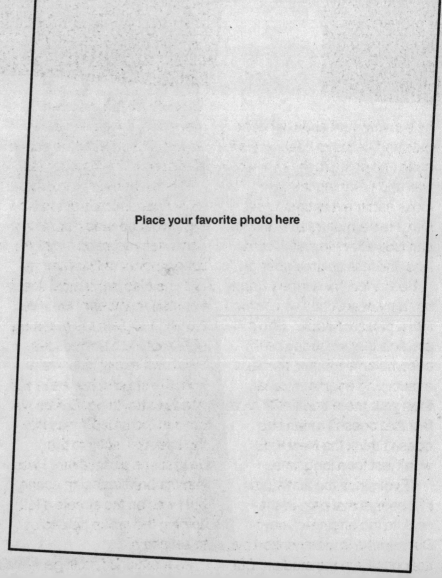

Place your favorite photo here

Danny with his mom and dad at the United Cerebral Palsy Telethon.
Robin Platzer

he's concerned about what he eats and he looks healthy. He is quite into going to the gym as well and pumping iron. He looks better every time I see him. He's a mature boy and he can look after himself. I worry less and less as time goes on."

Betty Wood describes Danny as "a pleasant child who turned into a pleasant adult." She still predicts that someday he'll become an engineer, perhaps a recording engineer rather than your more traditional type. But that doesn't mean she doesn't think the New Kids won't last for a long time.

"Ever since the first album, I've been a real pain-in-the-neck to the engineer," says Danny, who is mesmerized by the console in the studio. "But it's so much fun. You can do so many cool things—you can almost entirely alter the sound of the music being recorded."

While Danny is probably the most academically gifted New Kid (well, Joe runs a close second since he got on his high school honor roll last semester!), he also is the most street-oriented member of the Kids. Asked to explain the meaning of "street-kid," Danny says: "Well, we're city kids; we're from the streets, but we're not hoods or anything. Before we got into the group, I was into the streets—not into the drug scene or anything. I was into the breakdancing scene, but I was on the streets a lot. Joining the group helped us to set goals."

As mentioned, college

was the biggest thing other than personal time that Danny had to give up to join the New Kids and help propel them to stardom.

"I had a four-year academic scholarship to Boston University, but I couldn't really concentrate on that, because I wanted to do this so bad," says Danny. "I was going to the studio every day, because I was learning about engineering and I engineered two songs on *Hangin' Tough.* So I left school. My parents were totally against that. But I still have my scholarship and I can go back when I want. My father said, 'If you leave school, you have to get a real job.' So I was a courier, delivering airline tickets for about six months before 'Please Don't Go Girl' took off. Then I quit."

One thing that Danny didn't "quit" was his old friends. They still turn up at the shows and Danny is genuinely happy to see them. Danny says that all the New Kids' old friends are really proud of them. "Our real friends haven't changed. Sometimes you get people who try to be your friend even though they never wanted to hang around with you before."

Danny's got a "live and let live" philosophy towards life. He really doesn't plan too far ahead and he likes to enjoy every moment as he lives it. And there are plenty of things for him to enjoy in his life right now. Danny is the New Kid who seems to have accumulated

Danny takes care of himself by eating healthy foods and working out at the gym. *Ernie Paniccioli*

the most friends. He makes an effort to look up people before he reaches their town, calling them from a cellular phone either in a limo or on the tour bus.

Danny believes in clean living, and his idea of a good time is just to curl up in front of the VCR at the back of the tour bus. One of the movies he loves to watch is *Coming to America*—which he's seen about ten times. Not surprisingly, he tries to spread the good word about clean living to fans.

"I feel a strong responsibility to fans. Sometimes in the press, you hear jokes that we're squeaky clean. We're drug-free but it's not like we're wimps. Anyway, I do think it's important to set an example for teenagers because at that point in your life, you're dealing with some mega-heavy peer pressures. Drugs are a dead end. But yet some kids feel they have to do them to be 'in'. We want to change that way of thinking. Whoever said drugs were cool is a loser. They can kill you or make you lose your mind. I heard this saying once: 'Users are losers and losers are users…' That's just the way I feel."

How to sum up Danny Wood in a nutshell? Well, he's a guy who works hard and plays hard. Above all else, he's a good friend who's always there …and he can lift anyone's spirits. "He really cares about people," says Donnie with a smile, "and that's why we love our 'Puff McCloud'!"

Place your favorite photo here

IN FLIGHT WITH "JOE-BIRD" MCINTYRE

Born on December 31, 1972, Joe "Joe-Bird" McIntyre is the youngest member of the New Kids. What's so incredible about this young man is that

golden-brown curls

sparkling blue eyes

dazzling smile

Vinnie Zuffante, Star File Photo

fame appears not to have changed his outlook on life in the least. His oldest sister, Judy confirms, "He's still the sweet, innocent little brother I've always known."

Joe has always been a natural-born ham—as a grammar and junior high schooler, he performed in *Oliver* and in a Boston community theater production of *Our Town* (where he portrayed a dead person and had to sit still for an hour!). Joe's from a family where just about everyone sings, dances, or acts. It's always been a common occurrence for almost the whole clan to appear onstage together at the Footlight Theatre in their native Jamaica Plains, Massachusetts.

Sister Judy talks about Joe's younger days: "Joe was a sweet kid…he had eight people in front of him (in the family) so he was the baby and had a lot of nurturing."

Joe's earliest interest in show business, like for many other young stars, started on a local level: "In our family, whatever one of us does is accepted by the others. I sang and danced in the Neighborhood Children's Theater of Boston ever since I was six. In fact, in one show, our whole family sang except for my dad, who sat in the back row watching."

Like the other boys, Joe picked up his slick dance moves and singing style just

Joe and his dad during the Hangin' Tough Tour in 1989.
Robin Platzer

from hangin' out with the neighborhood kids, and his skills were honed in early '85 after he joined the New Kids. As the story goes, Joe auditioned on Father's Day, 1985, to replace Jamie—a friend of Donnie's whose parents were worried about him entering showbiz at such a young age. When Mary Alford came to pick Joe up and drive him to Maurice's house to audition, he was so nervous he couldn't even think straight. But Joe's audition was a smash and Maurice presented him with the three-record Motown selection, *Jackson Five Anthology*. This was an important gift, for Joe listened very closely to Michael Jackson's lead vocals which helped him develop his own unique style. (Joe usually performs a Jackson Five hit in concert and, needless to say, the audience goes wild!)

Joe is the only New Kid with musical theater in his background. When Joe first joined the New Kids, he was designated the lead singer or "Michael Jackson" of the group, but as time went on, the lead vocal duties were shared by the boys. Because Joe's voice changed right after "Please Don't Go Girl" was recorded two years ago, Joe has a tougher job singing live than the other Kids do. As a solution, the boys put the hit in a medley so that poor Joe doesn't have to make it through the whole four-minute song!

Place your favorite photo here

What was Joe's mom's reaction when he told her he wanted to become a professional singer? "I never thought about the future," Kay McIntyre responds. "I just never really have done that. I just thought, 'This is fun...he will do it, and he is working hard.' He was going to rehearsals at night in grammar school. When he was a freshman at Catholic Memorial, he got first honors all year. The night he got the academic award, I was so proud of him. I would love him to be a really good student and go to college."

Joe *has* talked about going to college and majoring in journalism when the New Kids get a significant amount of time off. "When I go to college, I want to concentrate on it. I'm just like that. I want to do well and fully commit myself. But I always feel that I'll be in the business one way or another."

Well, what about the future of the New Kids? Joe responds when asked if the group would ever change their name: "New Kids On The Block is just a collective name to call us. I don't think the name is an issue. If you're established, it doesn't matter (what your name is). We'll never shun the name New Kids On The Block."

Joe will never shun any of his old friends either, though all the Kids agree that sometimes it's hard to tell who's sincere and who just wants to be around them because they're famous. Mrs. McIntyre says that Joe makes a point of seeing all his old friends when he's home. "The few boys around here are boys that he has always known. He does make a point of seeing them. He is not a writer, but he will call them."

Joe's mom still tries to give him advice during the rare moments they have together, but overall, she trusts him to conduct himself in a mature and considerate manner when he's away on the road. "All I want you to be is kind," Mrs. McIntyre advises Joe. "Try to remember that people are people. If you're kind, then you won't hurt other people's feelings. That is what I want you to do."

Joe has taken his mom's advice, and his extreme kindness to those he meets on the road, especially fans, have made him turn up at the top of popularity polls conducted by dozens of teen magazines.

He's a team player who really knows how to give emotional support to others. No doubt about it—with his looks, talent, and personality, this "Bird" will be flying for a long time!

Joe juggles a regular high school schedule while on the road.
Vinnie Zuffante, Star File Photo

REPORTER'S EYE-VIEW "ON TOUR WITH NKOTB"

It's a thrill to be able to fly to a town and watch the New Kids prepare for a show. Spending a whole day with the Kids in New Orleans was a treat the author of this book recently enjoyed. What was so amazing to observe is that the guys have a lot of work to do before and after a show—not just *during* a show!

The New Kids' bus pulls in to the hotel around 1:00 p.m. (well, actually there are two buses, but one is for the crew).

They have just enough time to open their suitcases before being whisked to a TV station, interview, or photo session.

When we visited with the Kids in New Orleans (the Big Easy), they had to do one-on-one interviews with a dozen members of the European press who were flown in, and spent two hours talking to all the journalists and meeting their photo needs. Shortly thereafter, the guys had a quick

The guys have a lot of work to do before and after a show—not just while on stage.
Ebet Roberts

round of basketball—which is their usual way to unwind after a particularly stressful day.

At 4:00 p.m., as always, the Kids had to "soundcheck" for an hour. The soundcheck is their opportunity to test all the equipment and make sure there will be no technical difficulties during their show. Singers are especially concerned that their microphones are in order and that there will be no feedback through the speakers.

After soundcheck, the boys usually have a meeting with tour manager Peter Work—the guy who keeps the show on the road—and that's just what happened in New Orleans (the guys were performing at the University of New Orleans Lakefront Auditorium). The guys learned that the evening would be spent entertaining a girl who won a "Meet the New Kids Contest" and then meeting with a group of American teen magazine reporters who were there to cover the event.

Right before the show, the guys literally put their heads together to meditate. After five years, it not only is a tradition, but a method for staying close.

The New Orleans show was particularly stressful because of all the press and photo shoots the guys had scheduled that day and there was little

Even though each of the Kids has a different personality, they are great friends and enjoy spending their free time together.
Ebet Roberts

time for gathering thoughts before going onstage. As a matter of fact, Jon didn't even realize how close show time was and couldn't finish walking his Shar-Pei pup, Houston, so bodyguard Biscuit had to finish the pup's walk backstage.

The South has always been kind to the New Kids, and their concert at the UNO Lakefront Auditorium was particularly exciting. The boys can actually feel the audience's energy and enthusiasm which helps them to perform their best. When

Place your favorite photo here

they leave the stage, all the gifts and flowers are gathered up and sent to a local children's hospital or given to the United Cerebral Palsy office for distribution.

We reporters tried to corner the guys after the show, but fans come first. There were at least 100 kids who managed to get backstage and were lined up for autographs. The guys accommodated the fans while wearing the terry-cloth bath-robes that are standard after-show attire.

After spending a good hour with the fans, the boys got into long black limos. They were reluctant to actually depart—they just love those Southern accents—but they knew that the next night would be filled with new faces to meet. For guys who "hang tough," they're certainly "softies" for their fans!

Big smiles as the NKOTB show off their two American Music Awards.
Vinnie Zuffante, Star File Photo

Place your favorite photo here

Donnie, Danny and Jordan (left to right). The New Kids love their fans and credit them for their continued success.
David Seelig, Star File Photo

WHAT'S AROUND THE BLOCK?

Obviously, the guys have enough work with their forthcoming album, cartoon, feature film, and Christmas special. All this spring, they will be in Europe promoting their new album on tour and then coming back to the States for yet another concert tour.

Certainly, rumors about solo projects have been floating around—that happens with any big group. Joe lays the rumors to rest about solo projects: "Right now, we're just a really good team. I think everyone has just as much of a chance (to make contributions) as everyone else. We really go well together. We all have different personalities that attract different crowds of people—so we appeal to a *lot* of people. So, right now, we're not talking about solo projects. Even if we branch off—the other guys might go into production and stuff like that, and I want to go into acting—I think we'll always be known as the New Kids On The Block.

"I think we'll stay together. We're a really good team and we're proud of ourselves. And for a long while, we'll be think-

The Kids feel a strong responsibility to their fans and are proud of being positive role models.
Vinnie Zuffante, Star File Photo

ing about the group, not ourselves (as individuals)."

The guys plan to stay together for as long as possible, and there are absolutely no signs of boredom at this point. "This is also a brotherhood," says Donnie. "It goes way beyond just people who work together. You always read about rock stars who have separate tour buses and don't speak to each other when they're offstage. That seems so ridiculous to us. How could anyone put up with that situation? Everyone around you has to be your friend because you have to work *for* each other, not against each other. Plus, it could get kind of lonely on the road if you've got no one there with you who really cares about you.

"People always ask me if the affection we show for each other is real. Absolutely! I don't know where I'd be without these guys. We pool our energy and the New Kids happens."

It's Jordan who puts it best when he says that the fans are responsible for the New Kids' success. "We'd like to say thank you to all our fans for giving us the support we need, and we love all our fans. The New Kids will be there for you all the time."

The Kids' touring and recording schedule doesn't allow time for girlfriends.
Vinnie Zuffante, Star File Photo

NEW KIDS' ♡'N'✸ LOVES HATES

Just like anybody else, the New Kids have things they love and things they hate. Some are funny and some are serious, but one thing's for certain—by learning what someone really loves and hates, you *really* get to know them!

Danny Wood

LOVES:

• Girls in bikinis.

• All types of black music, from old-fashioned R&B to rap!

• Friendly people, especially the nice people he meets on the road. "A lot of musicians tell you what a bad place the road is, but honestly, you meet some really great people who show you around the town and stuff. It's cool."

• Being in the New Kids. "I hope this lasts forever. More important than our success or anything, though, is that we're good friends. I think we'll be friends forever."

• Spicy food, especially Mexican. "I really like to try all kinds of food, though, especially when we're in New York."

• Performing. "I live for going onstage. I still get nervous before each show, but when I hear the screams from the crowd, it really gets me excited and I wouldn't want to be anywhere else in the world."

HATES:

• Unfriendly people. "I don't know why everyone can't make an effort to be nice."

• Getting to a show late, and not getting a soundcheck. "I need to relax before a show. I hate being in a rush."

• People who say the group is only "a flash in the pan." "People who say stuff like that about us really haven't listened to our records closely. We really have a lot of talent I think."

• Finding out his favorite jeans are dirty when he's about to change into them!

Danny loves all types of music from old-fashioned R & B to rap.
David Seelig, Star File Photo

Donnie Wahlberg

LOVES:

• Being from a big family. "It's the best. There's always someone to hang out with, or talk about your problems with. You're never depressed."

• Girls who are understanding. "Any girlfriend of mine has to understand that I'm away a lot and that I have very heavy demands on me because of my career. Being in a group takes up 90 percent of my time and energy."

• Wearing casual clothes. "I guess I'm kind of a slob. I never like to dress up and I really love ratty, tattered jeans."

• Take charge kind of people. "That's because I'm that kind of person. I love to coordinate photo sessions and do all the talking in interviews."

HATES:

• Sound difficulties during a show. "You can't really avoid that, and we have great sound people who can deal with it when it happens."

• Fans who cut his hair. "That's going a little bit too far when someone sneaks up behind you and snips off a piece of your hair. It can definitely ruin a good haircut."

• Not getting enough sleep. "I'm a sleep freak, but you can't get more than five hours a night on the road. I dream about being at home and getting to sleep for as long as I want."

Donnie is sensitive and intense under that playful exterior.
Vinnie Zuffante, Star File Photo

Joe McIntyre

LOVES:

- Hearing the crowd's reaction. "I really get a rush when I hear all the screaming going on out there. It helps me to do my best when singing live. I wouldn't want to disappoint anyone."
- Hanging out with the guys. "We really are best friends. We're not just saying that."
- Comedian Jay Leno. "He's from Boston and we hang out sometimes. I love to watch him host *The Tonight Show.*"
- Oreo cookies. "It's my favorite afterschool snack."
- Meeting new people...especially if they're fans of New Kids On The Block.

HATES:

- Having to juggle between a regular high school schedule and a tutor while he's on the road—although he is an honor roll student at his Jamaica Plains high school.
- Heavy metal music. "It's a real clichéd kind of thing."
- Missing his friends when he's on the road. "I've got a lot of friends, and it's hard to keep up with all of them. I don't really have time to write letters, and I only have time for quick phone calls."
- Road food. "There are great places to eat in Boston, New York, or LA but other places are disappointing...well, in the South there's some great barbeque."

Joe "Joe-Bird" McIntyre has always been a natural born ham. *Ebet Roberts*

Jonathan Knight

LOVES:

• Recording. "I really love it in the studio and I have a fascination with all the technical stuff, like the control board. I'd like to be an engineer someday."

• Going out on long tours. "I love being able to travel. I especially loved when we used to play amusement parks because a lot of the time they'd close down the park for us so that we could go on rides after the show."

• Girls who are independent. "It's so important for a girl to be on her own and be able to take care of herself. That should be the case whether she's going out with someone seriously or not."

HATES:

• Missing his friends and family when he's on the road. "I know they'll always be there, though, even when I'm away for a long period of time. Sometimes relationships actually get stronger when you haven't seen someone for a while."

• Missing his music collection when he's on the road. "I have a big collection of tapes and I obviously can't take all of them out on the road with me. The collection probably weighs seventy pounds."

• People who don't like Boston. "Boston is the greatest town in the world. It's got everything from restaurants to a great zoo. And the public transportation system is the greatest."

Though Jon's been to a lot of places, he considers Boston the greatest town in the world.

Mike Quastella, Star File Photo

Jordan Knight

LOVES:

• Having his brother in the group with him. "Jon and I get along really great, although we have the occasional brotherly fight. We always make up, though."

• Playing basketball. "It's the whole group's favorite sport. I'd say that Donnie is the best player, though, 'cause he's really fast on his feet."

• Going shopping. "I really enjoy going to malls and looking for clothing and sneakers. It's relaxing."

• His mom, Marlene. "She's great. She helps take care of the fan mail and really supports me and Jon doing this."

HATES:

• Getting lost from the other guys. "Sometimes I'll go off and talk to some of the fans, and somehow get separated from the other guys. It's weird having to find your way around in a strange town."

• People who call the New Kids a "teenybopper group." "Those people don't totally understand us. I hate when people make generalizations like that. If they just listen to our albums, they can hear all different styles."

• Bad comedy movies. "I won't name any names, but the last few comedy films I saw were really turkeys."

Jordan says people who call the New Kids a "teenybopper" group just don't understand their music. *Vinnie Zuffante, Star File Photo*

NEW KIDS' FILL-IN QUIZ... FOR DIE-HARD "BLOCKHEADS" ONLY!

1. Who is the oldest New Kid?

_____

2. Whose nickname is Puff McCloud?

_____

3. What's the name of Jon and Jordan's mom?

_____

4. Whose mom was opposed to him leaving college to join the group? (Hint: He was best friends with Donnie.)

_____

5. How many copies of *Hangin' Tough* have been sold worldwide?

_____

6. What is the name of the New Kids' Christmas album?

_____

7. This New Kid won awards in high school for his painting and creative writing.

_____

8. Which New Kid is producing a local Boston rap group called "The Northside Boys"?

_____

9. Which New Kid has the most siblings?

_____

10. Which New Kid's voice changed shortly after recording "Please Don't Go Girl" and now he can barely sing it live in concert?

_____

11. Which network will premiere the NKOTB cartoon?

_____

12. What's the name of Jonathan's Shar-Pei puppy?

_____

13. What is Joe's favorite cookie?

_____

14. This New Kid's secret desire is to be in a movie with Eddie Murphy.

_____

15. What is the name of Donnie, Jordan, and Danny's production/engineering/songwriting team?

_____

16. Name the lovable and handsome New Kids tour manager.

_____

17. These two dudes are the New Kids' Mr. T-like bodyguards who sign almost as many autographs as the Kids do!

_____ and _____

18. Who is Donnie's role model?

_____

19. Which toy manufacturer is producing the Kids' dolls and other related merchandise?

_____

20. Who tells the audience to "love one another"?

_____

The Kids backstage at the Westbury Music Fair in New York.
Robin Platzer

Backstage at the American Music Awards in Los Angeles. Look for a NKOTB cartoon, new album and Christmas special this year. *Wide World Photos*

How Did *You* Score?

16–20 Right: You're "hangin' tough" alright! You deserve a lifetime backstage pass to the New Kids' shows—not to mention a kiss on the cheek from your favorite Kid. You're a real "blockhead."

10–15 Right: Not bad—but you can do a little brushing up on your New Kids facts. Why not re-read this book and then pick up a copy of *New Kids On The Block* by Anne M. Raso? You'll be a "blockhead" in no time.

5–9 Right: What, you didn't know that Robo and Biscuit were the New Kids' body-guards—or that Peter Work is their tour manager? Well, don't expect to go on the road with the NKOTB anytime in the near future. You've got a lot of brushing up on New Kids facts to do first. Give your copy of *Hangin' Tough* a few more spins while you're at it.

Below five Right: Are you *sure* you're a New Kids fan?

Answer Key
1. Jonathan Knight
2. Danny Wood
3. Marlene
4. Danny Wood
5. 10,000,000 +
6. *Merry, Merry Christmas*
7. Donnie Wahlberg
8. Donnie Wahlberg
9. Joe McIntyre
10. Joe McIntyre
11. ABC
12. Houston
13. Oreos
14. Jordan Knight
15. Crickets
16. Peter Work
17. Robo, Biscuit
18. Maurice Starr
19. Hasbro
20. Jonathan Knight

"BLOCKBUSTERS" A NEW KIDS DISCOGRAPHY

New Kids on the Block (Columbia Records)—Released December 1986 Features: "Stop It Girl"; "Didn't I (Blow Your Mind)?"; "Popsicle"; "Angel"; "Be My Girl"; "New Kids on the Block"; "Are You Down?"; "I Wanna Be Loved by You"; "Don't Give Up on Me"; and "Treat Me Right."

Singles released off this album were (in consecutive order):
"Be My Girl"; "Stop It Girl"; and "Didn't I (Blow Your Mind)?"

Hangin' Tough (Columbia Records)—Released March 1988 Features: "You Got It (The Right Stuff)"; "Please Don't Go Girl"; "I'll Be Loving You (Forever)"; "Cover Girl"; "I Need You"; "Hangin' Tough"; "I Remember When"; "What'cha Gonna Do (About It)"; "My Favorite Girl"; and "Hold On."

Singles released off this album were (in consecutive order):
"Please Don't Go Girl"; "You Got It (The Right Stuff)";

The Kids try to sign as many autographs as possible.
Robin Platzer

"I'll Be Loving You (Forever)"; "Hangin' Tough" (b/w "Didn't I (Blow Your Mind)?" from the first album); and "Cover Girl."

Merry, Merry Christmas (Columbia Records)—Released September 1989 Features: "This One's for the Children"; "Last Night I Saw Santa Claus"; "I'll Be Missin' You Come Christmas (A Letter to Santa)"; "I Still Believe in Santa Claus"; "Merry, Merry Christmas"; "The Christmas Song (Chestnuts Roasting on an Open Fire)"; "Funky, Funky Xmas"; "White Christmas"; "Little Drummer Boy"; and "This One's for the Children (Reprise)."

Singles released as of 9/89: "This One's for the Children."

Step By Step (Columbia Records)—Newest Album (Scheduled for May 1990 Release)

VIDEOGRAPHY

Short-form videos exist for all the singles. The Kids have released one long-form video (available from CMV Enterprises/CBS Music Video Enterprises), which is a compilation of the hit videos for "Please Don't Go Girl," "You Got It (The Right Stuff)," "I'll Be Loving You (Forever)"; and "Hangin' Tough." It was released in July '89.

Jordan and Jon with Tiffany who is now being guided by legendary NKOTB manager, Dick Scott. *Robin Platzer*

MAKE ALL YOUR DREAMS COME TRUE!

SUBSCRIBE TO *TEEN DREAM* FOR ONLY $15.00!
(That's A 15% Savings Over Newsstand Cost!)

Teen Dream is about to offer you one of the "dreamiest" deals ever! All you have to do to receive this hot bimonthly mag filled with tons of exclusive NKOTB pinups and feature stories is to fill out the coupon below and include a check for $15.00 ($18.00 for Canadian and foreign residents). Think about it — every other month, like clockwork, you will be receiving all the info and pin-ups you'll ever need on those ultra-tough New Kids, along with lots of scoops on all your other musical and Hollywood faves. There will be features on Paula Abdul, Fred Savage and Neil Patrick Harris just to name a few!

Published by Starline Publications, Inc., this is one teen mag you won't want to be without — as a matter of fact, it's the only one you'll ever need if you're a die-hard New Kids fan. So pick up a pen, fill in the coupon below, and off you go into "dreamland" — *Teen Dream* is a teen entertainment fantasy, 64 solid pages of fun 'n' fotos you'll never forget! Order now! (Don't miss out on this "way cool" offer!)

fabulous photos included

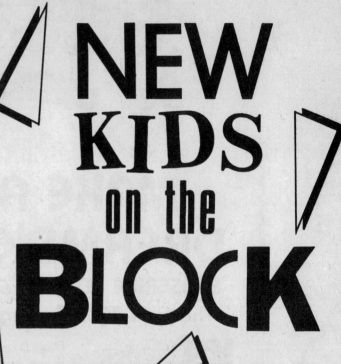

AMERICA'S FAVORITE POP GROUP AND THE HARDEST-WORKING KIDS IN SHOW BUSINESS!

Anne M. Raso, editor of *Teen Dream* magazine, has written a lively, first-hand and behind-the-scenes account of those fabulous boys from Boston. In this 64-page book, filled with great photos and interesting facts, you'll find out:

- how the group was "born"
- how they made it to the top
- how they feel about their families, their success, their future and each other!